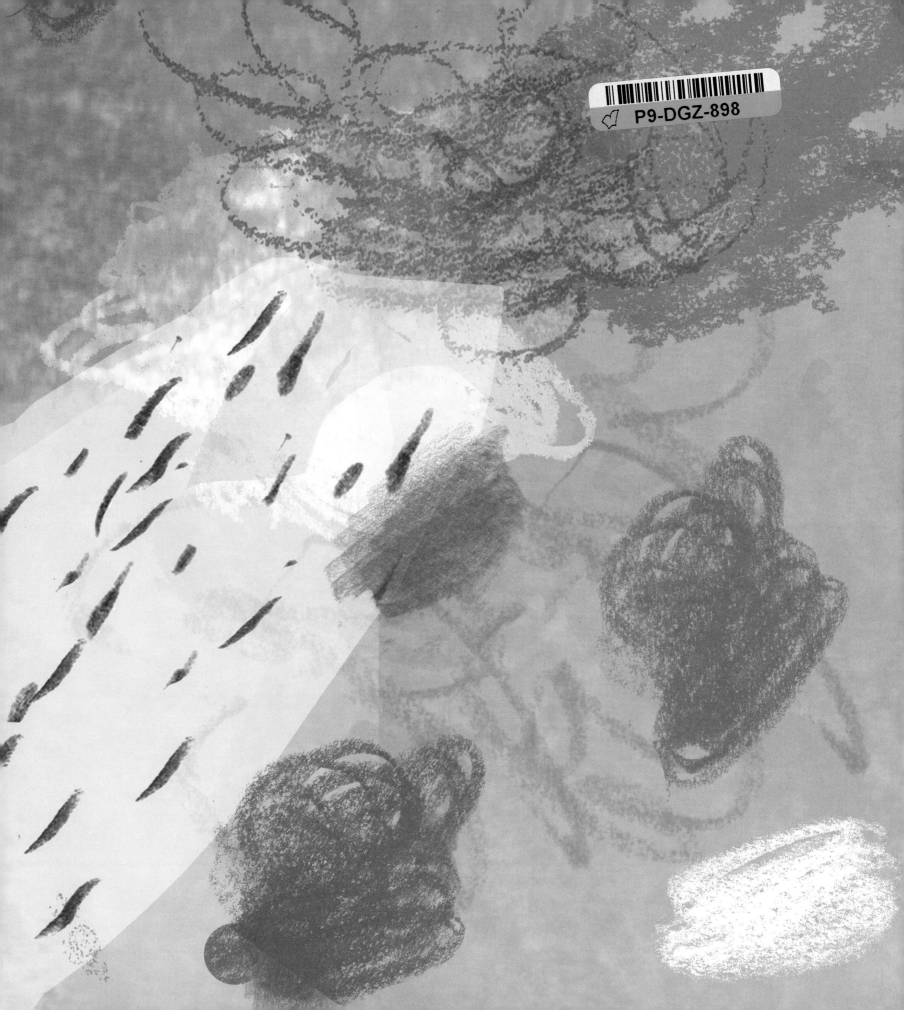

For Sam and Becky

First published in 2019 by Child's Play (International) Ltd
Ashworth Road, Bridgemead, Swindon SN5 7YD, UK

First published in USA 2019 by Child's Play Inc
250 Minot Avenue, Auburn, Maine 04210

Distributed in Australia by Child's Play Australia Pty Ltd
Unit 10/20 Narabang Way, Belrose, Sydney, NSW 2085

ISBN 978-1-78628-354-2
L210319CPL06193542

Printed in Heshan, China

1 3 5 7 9 10 8 6 4 2

A catalogue record of this book
is available from the British Library

www.childs-play.com

Astrid
and the
Sky Calf

Rosie Faragher

Here is Dr. Astrid.

And here
is her Hospital
for Magical Beasts.

With sticky tape...

and potions,

bandages and thread,

there's no creature she can't treat,
and no illness she can't cure.

One grizzly weather day,
a new patient arrives.

Dr. Astrid is excited to meet her first sky calf.

Hoping she can decide what's wrong,

Dr. Astrid asks, "Um, how can I help you?"

But Sky Calf can't explain what the matter is.

Certain she can figure it out,
Dr. Astrid gets to work.

She checks Sky Calf's
temperature, which
seems just right.

She listens to her heart,
which goes 'boo boom,
boo boom, boo boom.'

Maybe sticky tape will help.

But for once, Dr. Astrid's methods
are of no use. Everyone gets a little fed up.

Dr. Astrid
doesn't like
not knowing
what to do...

and it seems like Sky Calf
doesn't want to be fixed.

Dr. Astrid wonders if Sky Calf will leave.

But she seems to want to stick around.

Dr. Astrid wishes she could understand Sky Calf...

who seems very nice, after all.

Dr. Astrid gets Sky Calf to tell her where she comes from.

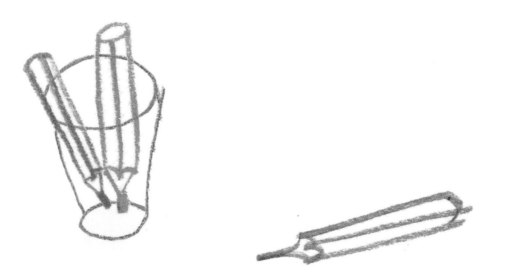

And for the rest
of the day...

she spends time keeping
Sky Calf company.

And just being her friend.

This makes things a lot better.

But Dr. Astrid wonders why sticky tape didn't work.

The next morning
Dr. Astrid goes to check
on her patients and gets
a wonderful surprise.

They are all having a lovely time with Sky Calf,
keeping each other company and being friends all together.

Dr. Astrid asks Sky Calf if she would like to stay and help with her Hospital for Magical Beasts.

She could do with an extra pair of hooves.

Sticky tape is all very well, she thinks,

but it's not the only way to make things better.